QUICK CHANGE

Tiny Tales of Transformation

DEBBIE YOUNG

About the Author

Debbie Young writes fiction and non-fiction in a multitude of genres from her peaceful Victorian cottage in a small village in Gloucestershire.

Now and again, she tears herself away from this rural idyll to search for adventure in the family camper van, accompanied by her husband and daughter.

Other excuses to escape from her desk include taking part in literary festivals, radio broadcasts and community events.

Blessed with a butterfly mind, she is never bored.

To keep up to date with Debbie Young's
new books and events, visit her website:
www.authordebbieyoung.com

Cover created by Debbie Young

from an original concept by SilverWood Books

www.silverwoodbooks.co.uk

ISBN 10: 0-9930879-6-5

ISBN-13: 978-0-9930879-6-7

Praise for Quick Change

"A book of tiny gems. Debbie Young's attention to detail brings the extraordinary out of the everyday."

Calum Kerr,

Author & Director of National Flash Fiction Day

"Very subtle, very English, very clever. I also loved the overall idea, the way the stories went from infancy to old age, shedding a revealing light on each stage. "

Marius Gabriel, author of The Original Sin

"Sly, witty, surprising, and the twists are genuine twists. The characterisation is lovely, very deft and economical. They make domesticity look edgy, sometimes dangerous, but they are also life-affirming."

Lucienne Boyce, author of To the Fair Land

QUICK CHANGE

Tiny Tales of Transformation

Dedication

For my high school English teachers,
who taught me that less can be more:
George Henning-Ross
& in memory of Joe Campbell
(Frankfurt International School 1974-78)

Contents

Out of the Mouths of Babes

Squinting in the hushed half-light of the hospital night-time, Judith rolled from her back on to her side, the lightness of her abdomen still a novelty. After months of feeling heavy, the absence of the baby curled up inside her would take some getting used to.

Not that the baby was far away. There it was, beside Judith's bed, silently sleeping in a transparent hospital crib. This functional contraption reminded her of a hotel laundry trolley, not at all like the pretty Moses basket awaiting its new occupant at home.

She gazed through the crib's plastic wall, trying to get used to how her baby looked. Peachy skin, button nose, rosebud lips, sparse blond down across the scalp: all standard baby issue. After nine months of staring at fuzzy monochrome scan images and cross-section diagrams in maternity guides, it was faintly surprising that her baby was in three-dimensional glorious Technicolor.

Her baby. My goodness, it really was her baby.

The baby was also taking time to adjust: eyes tight shut, limbs folded as neatly as Swiss Army Knife attachments, despite no longer needing to pack itself efficiently into the limited space inside Judith. But now the baby was on the outside, a tiny stand-alone human being.

So this is it, thought Judith: the first night of my child's life, my first night of motherhood, and the start of a relationship that can't be dissolved by divorce.

She could have done with more time to get used to the idea. On her way to the delivery suite for her Caesarean that morning, she'd suddenly remarked aloud: "I'm not sure I'm ready for this!"

The nurse escorting her had looked almost as alarmed as Judith's husband. Dave strolled anxiously alongside, clutching the knitted hat they'd been instructed to bring for the baby's debut. Judith hadn't realised newborn babies lost so much heat through their heads. There was so much still to learn.

"My dear, would you like to see a counsellor?" the nurse had asked, stopping Judith's progress with a gentle hand on her arm.

"It's a bit late now, isn't it?" Judith had exclaimed. "But don't worry, I'm not about to have a nervous breakdown. It just feels rather odd to think that when I leave theatre an hour from now, I won't be pregnant any more. And I'll have a baby. Giving birth is so final, don't you think?"

Fifteen hours on, as the ward clock ticked on into the night, Judith felt fraudulent laying claim to a baby. Despite the evidence in front of her, she felt as if she hadn't given birth at all. Caesareans, she mused, were about as close to natural labour as having your groceries delivered was to shopping in person at the supermarket.

Judith frowned. She was being silly. She wondered whether the drugs had not yet worn off. She had definitely witnessed the birth, albeit with a restricted view. A theatre assistant had erected a small green curtain across her middle, neatly matching the jovial surgeon's gown. The stage had been set for a dramatic entrance, but the curtains remained closed throughout the performance. For all she knew, Mr Peters could have left the baby inside her, simply tattooing stitches on her abdomen for effect.

Gingerly, Judith slipped one hand down to feel the incision from which Mr Peters had removed the baby as neatly as a letter from an envelope. No, it hadn't been all smoke and mirrors. She was definitely a mother. And the next day she'd be packed off home to get on with it.

"How am I going to cope?" she whispered, reaching out to touch the soft warmth of the baby's head for reassurance.

To her astonishment, the baby opened its deep grey eyes and turned them on Judith.

"What do you mean, how will you cope?" returned the baby in a small, high voice. "Haven't you ever heard of maternal instinct?"

Judith blinked hard twice, as if that might restore the scene to order.

"I'm sorry?"

"You're my mother. You'll cope. Mothers do. You'll know how."

"But I've never had a baby before. I've never even borrowed one to practise on."

She faltered, doubts flooding in. The baby fixed her with a knowing stare.

"You want me to give you proof? Then tell me how you feel when you look into my eyes."

Judith didn't know what she was going to say until she'd said it.

"I think you're the most beautiful thing I've ever seen. I never knew I could love anything this much. But don't tell your father. We don't want to hurt his feelings."

"Don't worry. Just keep saying how much I look like him, and he'll be fine."

Judith realised she was stroking the baby's hair in time with her heartbeat. She dared her forefinger to touch the soft patch on the top of its head. So soft, so vulnerable, so small.

With a sudden urge to pick the baby up, she swung her legs round to get out of bed, wincing at the incontrovertible evidence of her stitches. Leaning over the cot to scoop the baby up in her arms, she instinctively put one hand behind its head for support. Till that moment, she'd forgotten that she knew how to do that.

"Do you trust me to look after you, then?" she asked the baby. "Even though I'm new to this game?"

The baby gave a small smile, the sort that grandmas like to say is wind.

"Of course I do, you're my mother," said the baby. "We babies have instincts too, you know. You're my mother and you always will be, no matter how old and big I get."

"Do you know," said Judith, pressing the baby's face gently to hers and nuzzling into its neck, "I think you're right."

"Let's snuggle down and go to sleep now, shall we?"

The baby hiccoughed a little yawn, while Judith continued: "And in the morning, your father will take us both home."

"I'll wake you a few times between now and then," put in the baby, "because that's what babies have to do."

"That's fine," said Judith. "I understand that now."

"Of course you do," said the baby. "Now get some rest. I think you're going to need it."

Going to Grandma's

The trouble with being the youngest of three children is that whenever we travel anywhere by car, I always have to sit in the middle. It's bad enough when we're just going somewhere near home, but what's the worst thing in the whole wide world is when we go to Grandma's house. I get so squashed by my big brother Ben and my big sister Sarah that I'm as thin as a skittle by the time we get there.

It's always the same. We get onto the motorway and Mum says she's seen a sign that says something like "A hundred and thirty five zillion miles to Grandma's house". She thinks she's being funny, but actually it just reminds us that we've still got to drive about as far as the moon.

So I spread out a little bit, and Ben and Sarah start shouting to Mum about my elbows. Then Mum says something that's got nothing to do with it, like "Think how pleased Grandma will be to see us, darlings, so do be good". You have to wonder sometimes whether she really is in the same car as the rest of us.

Of course, that makes Ben and Sarah dig their elbows in me even more but without making any noise, so I have to start kicking them. It isn't my fault when my foot slips and kicks Dad's bum through the back of his seat.

Then Dad says "Right, that's it! I've had enough! I'm turning round and going home!" and swerves the car really hard so that Ben jerks sideways and his head hits Sarah's, over the top of mine (so I'm squished again) and it makes a big noise like dropping one of my wooden bricks on the kitchen floor.

Ben and Sarah go really quiet and go to sleep straight away, which surprises me, but Mum and Dad are too busy arguing to notice. I don't mind because it means I can now spread out as much as I like.

"Don't be so childish, Derek," Mum is saying, and Dad makes a grumpy noise and goes back to proper driving in a straight line the same shape as the road. He mutters something growly about "the trouble with your mother", and I'm not sure whether he's talking to us about Mum or to Mum about Grandma, but it makes me feel very sad.

By the time we get to Grandma's, Ben and Sarah have woken up again, though they look a bit funny and are very quiet. We all get out with our arms and legs not working properly, as usual, but I run about and laugh and joke because I'm really pleased to see Grandma.

Grandma says, "Ooh, you sound like you've had a fun journey!"

Dad rolls his eyes, and Mum slaps him on the arm to stop him saying anything. Then she gives Grandma a big hug with both arms, just like I hug Mum when she comes home from work and I've missed her ever such a lot, and I know we're going to have a lovely day at Grandma's after all.

Penny for Them

As Holly set down the old glass flagon on her bedroom windowsill, she was glad that she'd thought of such a good use for it. Now her mum would have to allow her to keep it, even if it did make dusting harder.

She began to drop into the empty jar the contents of a small plastic coin bag, given to her earlier that day by her grandpa. Each coin made a pleasing clink as it hit glass at the bottom, marking the start of her new saving system to enable her to buy the new phone she wanted. Its asking price was beyond her pocket money budget.

Grandpa saved all his copper coins for her. Every night, when he got home from work, he emptied his pockets, keen not to distort the sharp lines of his dark accountant's suits with shrapnel, as he called small change. Grandma had no use for copper coins either. She paid for everything by card, shopping largely online, with everything delivered to her door. It had been Grandma's idea to pass the coins to Holly when she visited every Saturday.

If only she had found the old flagon earlier, thought Holly, and saved all the pennies Grandpa had ever given her, how much richer she would be now! In the past, whenever he'd slipped a money bag into her hand, she'd spent its contents at the earliest opportunity, annoying the local sweet-shop by paying for her haul entirely in pennies.

Holly tilted the jar from side to side and watched the pennies slide about. If she'd saved all those other pennies, she'd already have bought that new phone! Now she'd have to wait till the jar was full. But still, the trusty old flagon would be her inspiration to save.

Holly's scheme was given an extra boost the next Saturday when Grandpa gave her not one but two bulging money bags. He'd been travelling a lot that week, gathering more change every time he bought a coffee. Holly wondered whether he'd been making an extra effort to save up coins, now that he knew she wouldn't be frittering them away on sweets.

Week by week, the level in the flagon steadily rose. Holly celebrated milestones along the way: the first time she could no longer see a space at the bottom of the flagon; when it was a quarter full; half full; reaching the bottom of the handles. It was nearly a year before the coins reached its neck, and then Holly needed both hands to empty the flagon onto the rug to be counted.

As the coins cascaded to deliver her jackpot, Holly felt a flutter of excitement in her tummy. She took out a dusty wooden chessboard that had been lying neglected in her toy cupboard (or games cupboard, as she kept forgetting to call it now she was too old for toys), and stacked coins worth exactly £1 on each of the sixty-four squares. OMG, she was going to be rich! Having filled the board, she extended the grid with further rows, till there was another whole chessboard's worth of coins.

She ran out of coins after making a hundred and twenty-nine stacks, and had forty-seven pennies left over. She was still more than eighty pounds short of her target. Surely not! She counted the rows again, wishing she'd misremembered her times table. She did not want to believe the inevitable truth.

If Holly hadn't thought herself so grown up, she would have cried. The coveted new phone was still out of reach. Who'd have thought you could have so much money and still be poor?

But she refused to be downhearted. She set the empty jar back on the windowsill and took a stash of empty coin bags from her knicker drawer. She slipped each neat stack of coins into a plastic coin bag, folded over the top of each one and tucked it into the drawer. She pursed her lips. To get the phone she wanted, she'd have to start filling the flagon all over again.

Closing the drawer with a clunk, Holly bent down to pick up the leftover coppers. As she posted them slowly back into the flagon, she wondered how long it would take to refill the jar.

But then an inspiration hit her. Perhaps she could ask Grandpa to save silver coins for her too? She didn't think he'd miss the odd 5p. Or 10p, or 20p. She straightened her back and smiled.

Good old Grandpa! If she asked him nicely, surely he'd be happy to help? Congratulating herself on her resourcefulness, she tipped the flagon upside down into her palm, the forty-seven pennies spilling out in a rush. Then she skipped off to the sweetshop to spend them.

The Metamorphosis

One day, a small red-spotted caterpillar covered with short, dark hairs took up residence on the teenage boy's bedroom ceiling. It curled up like a Quaver in the angle where the ceiling met the wall.

Every afternoon, after he came home from school, Marcus would lie on his bed, staring idly up at the caterpillar, hoping to share its metamorphosis.

As the days passed, it slowly wrapped itself in silver thread, spinning a fuzzy cocoon.

One Thursday afternoon, while Marcus was sprawled on his bed, he caught sight of a new mirror that his mother had affixed to his bedroom wall during one of her furtive tidying missions when he was at school. Heaving himself upright, he strolled over to examine it. His reflection showed him numerous red spots lurking beneath short, dark stubble curling around his lower jaw. His gasp of horror hinted at the changes that had been taking place in his voice the last few weeks. It had the ratchetty undercurrent of a cricket's song.

From his desk, Marcus grabbed his pencil case and lobbed it angrily at the cocoon. It plummeted to the floor and lay motionless, blameless, patient, its occupant almost certainly dead. Shaken by the impact of his impetuous act, the boy took flight in his own way, careering from his house to the skate park.

Peep Behind the Curtain

The moment she drew the curtain of the changing room behind her, Imogen regretted entering the cubicle. She'd forgotten how harsh the lights were; how close and unforgiving the vast mirrors that imprisoned shoppers at their most vulnerable.

Imogen had been avoiding clothes shops for months. Till the current heatwave had taken hold, she'd got by with her old winter faithfuls, but there was only so long you could wear boots in the spring without looking like a time traveller with faulty navigation. She needed to invest urgently in a summer wardrobe to keep in with the girls at the office.

The telesales team at Blenkinson's Catering Supplies favoured the fashions purveyed by the Stacey Smiley chain. In the canteen last Monday, Lily Gray, the team's self-appointed style guru, had whisked out a new dress from the familiar purple carrier bag initialled "SS", to the predictable oohs and aahs of her colleagues.

"Stacey Smiley's is the only place to go these days if you want to be bang on trend," Lily had pronounced, patting her laboriously straightened hair.

The phrase "bang on trend" always sounded clumsy to Imogen. It made her think of models falling off high heels, landing on the catwalk with a thump. But, not wanting to look different from the other office girls, she headed the next Saturday to Stacey Smiley's.

Feeling conspicuous under the gaze of idling shop assistants, she browsed the rails in hope of finding something vaguely tolerable.

She wondered, why couldn't she love clothes shopping, as the other girls seemed to? Maybe it was because she didn't fit as easily as they did into Stacey Smiley's cheap sweatshop-made clothes. Imogen was neither fat nor unhealthy; she just had a squarer frame than the average customer's. While she certainly did not aspire to have a waist like a Barbie doll, she wouldn't have minded slipping as easily into fancy clothes.

This season she'd be at an extra disadvantage. She realised as she circuited the shop that the current must-have colours, bright primaries in solid blocks, would not at all suit her pale skin and fair hair. She sighed. All the other girls in the office would be wearing them.

Homing in on royal blue as the least objectionable shade, she amassed an armful of tops, trousers and skirts, and headed to the changing rooms. An unsmiling assistant, guarding the entrance like Cerberus, doled out a plastic tag to indicate the maximum number of garments allowed, and pointed towards the nearest vacant cubicle. Imogen flung the clothes on the flimsy red chair crammed into the corner, before pausing to appraise herself in the wall of mirrors. She hoped the familiar sight of her reflection would bring courage. It did the opposite.

Sighing, she picked up a flared skirt from the top of the pile and tried it against her waist. She didn't need to try it on to know it would add inches to her hips. On a whim she held the fabric to her face. Its instant effect of making her look half dead was strangely familiar. Of course! It was the same colour as her old school uniform, another sartorial nightmare banished from her life five years before.

With a gasp of horror, Imogen let the skirt fall to the floor. God, what was she thinking, allowing Stacey Smiley to fill the vacancy left by the school outfitters? What on earth was she doing here? It was high time she started wearing what she wanted to wear, not what someone else dictated, and it wouldn't be in primary colours. She'd always fancied that vintage shop along the high street, but never had the courage to cross the threshold. Now she would.

Before she could change her mind, Imogen gathered up the gaudy pile of clothes, swept aside the cubicle curtain and stalked with new confidence down the aisle to the waiting assistant.

"That was quick," the woman said flatly, taking the clothes.

"Yes," said Imogen, flashing a smile of relief. "And I can't tell you how pleased I'm going to be with my new look."

The Art of Medicine

"But, doctor, I really need my eyebrows tattooed on the National Health," the girl is saying, leaning too far forward on his consulting desk and digging her long fake nails into its leather top.

It's not for nothing that Dr Edwards has subconsciously built a little fence of drugs companies' promotional stationery between the edge of his desk and the patient's chair. Fluorescent bulldog clips are aligned like castellations along a wall of branded pens.

Struggling to remain civil, the doctor counts ten seconds, gazing at a bright yellow alarm clock, gifted to him the day before the regulations changed, banning reps from giving branded gifts to doctors. Although he'd always dreaded to think how much such gifts were adding to the nation's drugs bill, a small part of him was disappointed at the new ruling. He clung on to his ageing supplies like a comfort blanket.

"I'm afraid over-plucked eyebrows don't really count as a medical need," he says carefully, trying not to look at Natasha's naked browbones. "It's simply cosmetic."

"My nan had cosmetic surgery on the NHS last year."

"Your nan had reconstructive surgery after a mastectomy. That's rather different."

"Well, what about my stress levels? I'm getting stressed out going round looking like this. Think of how much money it'll save you in anti-depressants if I have my eyebrows tattooed on the NHS."

For a moment she looks triumphant.

"I'm not prescribing you anti-depressants. You're not depressed. Just over-plucked. They're eyebrows. They'll grow back."

Natasha drums her meticulously patterned nails on the desk as if warming them up for action.

"I'd like a second opinion. I'm going to get your

receptionist to give me an appointment for a second opinion. I know my rights."

She draws herself up on tall, narrow heels which beat an aggressive rhythm across the lino. The barbed wire tattoo around her left ankle adds to the feeling of threat. Once she's on the other side of it, she slams the door so hard that the latch of the coded lock falls shut with a snap.

Dr Edwards sighs and slumps back in his chair for a moment. Then, pulling himself together, he leans forward to peel off a small square of fluorescent pink paper from the jotter left six years before by an anti-depressant rep.

"How appropriate!" he murmurs.

From his anti-siege stationery wall, he selects a pencil branded with a hormone replacement. With a few deft strokes, his skill born of long practice, he sketches a recognisable outline of Natasha's face, or at least how it would look without her habitual heavy eyeliner, clogged mascara and flesh-plumping lipstick. He omits Natasha's temporary fix to her problem: stark brows painted on to tide her over till a tattooist is unleashed at the nation's expense. Instead, he carefully restores in light pencil marks as soft as a kiss the natural growth of her eyebrows. His version of Natasha is as pretty as a picture, as she used to be herself before her teenage hormones kicked in.

He sits back, holding up the sketch at arm's length, and allows himself a small smile at his pencil surgery.

"Another miracle cure!" he announces to the hypertension remedy teddy bear at his elbow, before reaching down to open the bottom drawer of his desk.

He drops the sketch from desktop height and it flutters down, spinning like an autumn leaf through warm, antiseptic surgery air. The tiny portrait lands, lopsided, at the top of a six inch pile of paper scraps, each of them bearing the doctor's sketch of a patient. Natasha's face falls onto one of last week's cases: young Alex, whose foot went gangrenous after a motorbike accident, requiring amputation when all else failed. The doctor's picture shows Alex scoring a goal in a football game, both feet still very much intact. Beneath Alex is an obese twelve-year-old, slimmed to perfect size by the trimming lines of his pencil: liposuction without the mess, Dr Edwards likes to think. A few inches further down is Natasha's nan, sporting a perfect pair of Page Three breasts as if they'd never been removed in his quest to save her life.

"Ah, the wonderful art of medicine!" says Dr Edwards. "By the power of my pencil, I declare you all cured."

He slams the drawer shut, another case closed.

"If only," he murmurs as he hits the buzzer on his desk to summon the next patient.

The Alchemy of Chocolate

If you dip a wafer biscuit into a chocolate fountain enough times, eventually it won't fit in your mouth. Much the same had happened with Jennifer's body. It was as if every bar of chocolate that she'd ever eaten had been melted down and painted onto her frame.

Oozing into hidden places, the fat encroached so gradually at first that Jennifer was slow to notice her transformation. Then, one summer's day while sunbathing on her lawn, she realised that she'd no longer pass the fat test that she and her friends had used at school: the ability to lay a ruler flat across her hipbones. (That was the best use they'd found for their geometry sets).

By the time she came to squeeze into an old pair of cords for Bonfire Night, Jennifer observed that where her stomach had once been concave, it now billowed out like a ship in full sail. No wonder sleeping on her tummy had become uncomfortable.

Trying on a party dress for New Year, she spotted that her waistline only curved inwards when elasticated clothing constrained her flesh.

By the spring equinox, the fat had found new places to hide. Her eyelids were thicker, and when inserting an earring, she had to push harder before the post emerged on the other side of the lobe.

Jennifer was glad when spring sunshine came early, because it gave her licence to go bare-legged. Lately, tights had become irksome. Unless she aligned the waistband precisely with that of her knickers, skirt and petticoat, her silhouette resembled the scalloped edge of a doily on a plate of cakes.

At Easter, Jennifer was quick to remove the temptation of her Easter eggs – by eating them. But then, at last, she decided to take action about her surplus fat. Precisely what action, she was not sure. She was unwilling to relinquish chocolate, or indeed any kind of food. Nor did she fancy exercising her way into shape. Poring over a list of how to burn calories, she was horrified by the ridiculous distance she'd have to run to work off a single bar of Dairy Milk. There had to be an easier way. It was just a question of dispersing fat rather than storing it.

Then, lulled to sleep on Midsummer's Eve by an exceptionally delicious hot chocolate, Jennifer had a remarkable dream. She dreamed of the perfect recipe for weight loss.

Next morning on waking, she knew exactly what to do. She rushed downstairs to her kitchen and assembled in a mixing bowl the ingredients dictated by her dream. Instead of stopping to wonder how this magical formula could require only store-cupboard staples, she got on with beating the mixture, her wooden spoon a biscuit-coloured blur.

Once the batter was blended, she tipped it into a saucepan and set it over a low heat, chanting the mantra that had also come to her in the dream. When the mixture was as smooth and warm as the perfect waistline, she decanted it into a jug and popped it in the fridge. She knew instinctively that this was the correct next step.

When she arrived at her office for work, she was so impatient for nightfall – the witching hour, or so her dream had told her – that she could hardly concentrate on her job.

As soon as she arrived home, she slipped on her nightie, took the jug from the fridge and with a medicine spoon measured out the dose prescribed in her dream. She swallowed the quivering spoonful in a rush, before she could change her mind, and retired to bed to await the results. The anxious fluttering in her tummy didn't stop her from tumbling into solid, dreamless sleep.

Waking next morning, she climbed out of bed, slipped off her nightdress and flung it distractedly on the bed. Reaching with her right hand behind the back of her neck, she grasped what the previous night's dream had told her she would find just above the nubbly bone at the top of her spine: a trapezoidal zip-pull. She grasped the metal.

Bending her head forward to clear her long, dark hair out of the way, Jennifer tugged the zip-pull between thumb and forefinger as far as she could. Then she stretched her left hand up behind her back to meet the right one, and continued pulling the zip down, slowly, slowly, until it reached the base of her backbone.

As the zip-pull stopped abruptly at her coccyx, the thick flesh covering Jennifer's upper back and shoulders started to feel loose. Soon she was easing off the entire outer casing of flesh as instinctively as a snake sheds its skin. Wriggling her hips and thighs to dislodge this pudgy onesie, she sat down on the bed, peeled it off her calves and finally stepped out of it on to the bedside rug.

Only now did she have the courage to glance in the dressing table mirror. There, to her delight, in a flawless casing of fresh skin, was her slender teenage outline. It was like meeting a long-lost, much-missed friend.

Glancing down at the discarded Jennifer-shaped fat that lay perfectly still on the floor, she wondered what on earth to do with it.

But of course! It was recycling day. She could simply put it in the green wheelie bin. After all, it should compost down as readily as bacon rind. Better to throw it in the wheelie bin than put it out in the garden for the birds.

With a new lightness of tread, Jennifer took a few steps around the bedroom. She felt decidedly different. The top of her thighs no longer rubbed together, her arms lay straighter against her sides, and she no longer felt that her stomach had been lagged, like the insulating jacket wrapped round a hot water tank.

Beginning to enjoy the full effect, Jennifer turned this way and that. But it wasn't the slim reflection in the dressing-table mirror that caused her to smile. It wasn't the realisation that her low-cost recipe would fetch a fortune on the heaving market for diet products. Nor was it the recognition that she'd achieved every slimmer's dream of alchemy, turning fat into gold. It was the thought that she could now eat as much chocolate as she liked, without ever having to worry about gaining weight. It was a dream come true.

The Impressionists

"Ellie Barker, fancy bumping into you here!"

The woman is so close that I can smell her cheap too-scarlet lipstick.

"Sorry?"

"Ellie, it's me! Sophie Hurst! Don't you remember? I used to sit next to you in Art at Westway Girls' High. We studied this very painting for our A Level. What would Mrs Salmon say if she knew?"

"I'm sorry, I think you're mixing me up with someone else," I say, as politely as I can. "I don't know a Mrs Salmon."

"No, of course, she was still Miss Jackson when we were in her class. I kept in touch after we left. She got married soon after. God, her art trips were such a laugh, weren't they? She never guessed about that vodka in my water bottle - still thinks I get travel sick on coaches."

"No, sorry, my name's Lisa Da Vinci..."

"And don't you remember how I pinched those postcards in the museum shop at the end? All those male nudes! God, how we laughed! God, I loved Art! Still do!"

She guffaws. One shouldn't guffaw in a gallery. I glance across to that Jeeves of the art world, the uniformed security man, who is sitting, arms folded, by the archway that leads to the Pre-Raphaelites.

"No, I'm sorry, you're mixing me up with someone who looks like me."

I moderate my voice to a much lower pitch, hoping she'll take the hint, but she thuds her outsized bottom down to sit right beside me, her scruffy jeans touching my linen trousers. I don't like anyone sitting so close to me, so I back away as far as I can without falling off the end of the black velveteen banquette. One wouldn't wish to appear undignified.

As she stares quizzically at me with narrowed eyes, I notice how her silver eye-shadow has fallen into leaden creases. It's not a good look.

"Really? Are you sure? I was just about to go to the cafe. If you'd been Ellie Barker, I'd have asked you to join me. Catch up on old times. Can't beat old friends, you know."

And with that she heaves herself off the bench and stalks off. I wait till the click-clacking of her precarious heels has faded across the parquet to a safe distance, down the stone stairs to the basement cafe.

I close my eyes for a moment, hoping to reboot my visual settings. I'd like to erase that awful made-up face and tarty clothes, and restore my contemplation of the ungilded beauty of Monet's Water Lilies. But it's no good. She's broken the spell.

I get up to leave, annoyed that I must now go elsewhere than the museum cafe for my luncheon. I cannot contemplate sharing a table with Sophie Hurst, who is likely to force herself on me. She'll be sure to eat with her mouth open, and if she bothers to use a napkin, she'll call it a serviette.

As usual, as I pass the security guard, I slip him a smile of approval. Unlike some of the riff-raff who pass through here, I'm sure he appreciates the finer things in life.

To my surprise, he holds up his hand to prevent my exit. "Just a moment, ma'am, I think you've left something of yours on the seat."

His voice is low, library-reverential, as it should be. We know how to behave in the presence of art.

He points to a small, shiny rectangle, conspicuous against the matte bench seat. Courteous, he rises from his seat to fetch it, his highly-polished brogues silent across the floor.

"Your Museum Friends card, I think?"

He peers at the card to check its details. The light in here is dim to preserve the art.

"Miss Barker?" he reads, frowning at me.

Ah. I cast my eyes down at his shoes. Goodness, his shoes are shiny.

"Yes, that's me."

"But you just told that woman your name's Da Vinci? Perhaps I'd better hand this in to Lost Property."

"No, no, it is I. I can prove it."

I produce from the pocket of my smock my Giaconda wallet, a souvenir of my recent trip to the Louvre, and flip it open. My driving licence photo-card clearly bears my image and my name: Eleanor Barker.

The security guard fixes me with an accusing look, the sort normally reserved for idiots who lean too close to a painting across the silken rope. I have to confess my fraud.

"Oh, all right. I admit it, I recognised her. But she was such a bore at school. I'm damned if I'm going to be her friend now. That's why I pretended to be someone else."

To my relief, his reaction is to smile.

"Don't worry, love, your secret's safe with me, madam," he says, tapping the side of his nose conspiratorially. "After all, this is the impressionists' gallery."

Patient Virtue

From beneath the crumpled duvet, I detect the sound of my husband's key in the front door. I flash a panicked glance at the bedside clock. What the hell's Patrick doing home so early?

Jeremy's heart pounds against my chest. No time to lose! I launch him out of bed with a shove.

"Quick, pretend I'm ill!" I hiss.

He grabs at the pile of clothes he's left on the bedside rug, slips his arms into his shirt and seizes his trousers from where they've been creasing my dress.

As Patrick's slow, heavy footsteps ascend the stairs, Jeremy's stuffing both legs at once into his trousers, feet into still-tied shoes. As he zips up his flies, I pull the duvet up to my chin to hide the fact that I am still naked, thank you very much. I fling my head dramatically back on the pillows, as if flaking out with a fever. Fortunately, my cheeks are quite flushed.

The bedroom door swings open and Patrick chucks his briefcase on the bed as if staking a claim. He does a double-take when he spots Jeremy lurking by my dressing table.

"Doctor, what are you doing here?" Patrick blurts, looking stupidly from Jeremy to me.

To divert attention from the bedside rug, where his tie is a pool of scarlet silk on my black knickers, with a flourish Jeremy pulls out a thermometer from his top pocket. He shakes it vigorously. He is a vigorous sort of a man. Then he clears his throat.

"Never too busy for a home visit, not for my golf partner's wife, Patrick! She wasn't really up to driving to the surgery. This new twenty-four-hour diarrhoea and vomiting virus is fierce when it starts to take hold."

Patrick falls for it, thank God.

"I thought she seemed alright when I left for the office this morning. Oh well, if you give me her prescription, I'll catch the chemist before it closes. Got time for nine holes later? It's a lovely evening for a quick round. I'll stand you a pint

afterwards too, to say thanks for giving my wife such special treatment."

A touch too hastily, Jeremy agrees, then obediently pulls a prescription pad out of his trouser pocket. He scribbles on it, signs the bottom and hands it to Patrick.

"These pills will bind her up in no time," he tells him heartily, without so much as a glance in my direction.

My heart sinks. I'm going to have to take them or our cover is blown. But still, constipation's a smaller price to pay for my fling than a divorce.

The Mutton and the Lamb

The sequins spelling out "Justin Bieber" across the woman's crop top are in a shade of silver that exactly matches her hair, but this dubious fashion statement is lost on the two teenage girls who are staring at her from within the cosy confines of the bus shelter. Their gaze is transfixed by her bare white blue-veined thighs. Combined with the scarlet mini skirt, the effect is that the components of the Union Jack are waiting to be properly assembled.

Stumbling on too-tight wedge-heeled red sandals, she approaches the bus stop. The darker of the girls pulls a tasteful lavender cashmere wrap more closely about her shoulders, although it is not cold that has made her shiver.

The woman judders to a halt before them, as if she's inadvertently put her shoes into neutral. From behind bifocals, she flashes a smirk at the cashmered girl.

"So, darling, now you know how it feels when someone borrows your favourite clothes without asking."

Glancing sideways, the teenager clocks her companion's dropped jaw. Then she sighs and peels off the lavender wrap.

"Ok, Mum, I get the message. Now, for God's sake go home and put your own clothes on."

Time Out

The seventeen years since their last meeting has not diminished their mutual attraction, although it has doubled their age.

At first shyly monosyllabic, they're soon bantering in the bar where they'd arranged to meet. They've easily picked up where they'd left off, destined for different universities at the age of eighteen.

Halfway through some inconsequential sentence, he can resist no longer. Leaning across the gap between their bar stools, he takes her face gently between his damp palms.

She replies to his lingering kiss: "Those seventeen years might just as well never have happened."

Unfortunately, his wife and two children had.

51

Clean Linen

There's nothing like a clean white shirt on a man, I always think. Ever since I married Graham, I've taken a pride in the state of his clothes when he goes off to work, and there's not much that satisfies me like a row of clean white shirts on the washing line.

I like all kinds of housework, and I'm pretty efficient at it – after all, I've had a lot of practice. I don't understand how some women find time to go to work or raise a family. Each morning I can't wait to pack Graham off to work so that I can start. I keep a duster and a can of Pledge by the front door so that, the minute he leaves, I can snatch it up and get straight on, doing a grand tour of all the rooms before I get the hoover out for another circuit.

Pledge has to be the favourite weapon in my armoury, which, I have to say, is a powerful one. You should see my broom cupboard - I have seventeen different cleaning products in there, and I'm proud to say I use every one every single day.

No shortcut is worth taking when it comes to house-work, but I do believe in trying to make life a little easier for myself. I keep the place tidy, and wash the pots the minute I've finished using them to avoid the risk of spills. I use only the purest, clearest soap and shampoo in the bathroom, and I gave up wearing make-up a long time ago - it was just a constant source of anxiety as to whether I'd end up with a smudge of rouge on a blouse or cardigan, and as to nail varnish – well, I wouldn't have it in the house.

Of course, that's not to say the dirt doesn't come sneaking into my house when I'm not looking. Take last night, for example. Graham came home, rather later than usual. His dinner was quite dried up in the oven by the time he sat down to eat it, but it didn't seem to bother him particularly. He wolfed it down, and seemed anxious to get out of the kitchen to go and get changed. But he didn't escape before I'd noticed the scarlet smudge on his collar as I leant over his shoulder to sweep his plate and cutlery away to the washing-up bowl.

"Goodness gracious me!" I exclaimed. "Is that lipstick on your collar?"

Graham opened his mouth but said nothing.

"You just take that shirt off this minute!" I cried. "I must get it in the wash before it stains! After all, I don't want people thinking I neglect my husband's needs."

He slipped it off as quickly as he could, ripping off one of the cuff buttons in his haste, and left the room at a run. I sometimes wonder why he isn't more grateful to have such a devoted wife.

(This story was first published in Flash Flood, the online journal for National Flash Fiction Day 2013.)

Domestic Blisters

Harriet's life began to change the day she gave up ironing.

That was also the day her husband Bryan had finally left her. It was a Tuesday. She'd always remember that because it was recycling day, and when she heard the sound of the bin man outside the front door, she'd thought it was Bryan coming back again. Bryan always used to put out the recycling.

To her surprise, her first thought when she realised that Bryan wasn't returning was that she'd have to put out the recycling herself in future. It was the only household chore for which he'd ever taken responsibility. He had strong views about recycling, as his constant monitoring of her kitchen waste bin made clear.

Her second thought was relief that she'd no longer have to get the creases just right in his suit trousers, or button his shirts when she put them on the hangers to keep the collars "set", as he called it. Bryan was always very particular about his clothing.

In his absence, Harriet decided not to bother ironing just for herself. What a liberating time-saver that would be! Then she realised that if she was clever about it, she wouldn't need to do much washing either. She didn't sweat the way he did, so her clothes lasted longer between washes.

A few weeks on and she realised she could even get away without getting dressed in the mornings. After all, who would know? She'd heard a new report that women went shopping in their pyjamas. It said so on BBC Radio 4, so it had to be true. And she hated the kind of clothes he'd allowed her to wear – skirts always below the knee; collars up to the chin. She might as well have been a nun and have done with it.

Nor was there any need to hoover or dust, now there was no-one around to run his finger, tutting, along the top of the piano or to drop mud from his shoes across the carpet and then complain about the mess.

Not having to cook would save her a lot of time too. No point in cooking a proper meal for one, was there? Ready meals would do, and she could get them delivered by the supermarket to her door. And that would save on washing up, as she could just eat them straight out of the packet (not worth dirtying plates) and bin the empties. Bin. In the black bin, not the green one. Of course, Bryan would have insisted she wash and recycle the plastic, and tuck the cardboard sleeves into the green bin.

Harriet hugged herself with delight as she put her first Mariner's Pie wrapper in the black bin. How could something so wrong feel so right?

Six weeks after Bryan had left, she was cleaning her teeth in front of Bryan's shaving mirror when she noticed her hair was untidy. She couldn't remember where she'd last seen the hairbrush. Had she even used it since he'd gone? Now that he wasn't there, nagging her to pin it up into a bun every day (he hated short hair on a woman, but didn't like long hair loose either), she simply hadn't bothered.

She gazed thoughtfully around the bathroom. Where could that hairbrush have gone? Her eyes alighted on the pair of beard-trimming scissors she'd bought as a hint that Bryan should trim his eyebrows and nose-hair. Pulling them out of their unopened wrapping, she decided to solve the problem of the missing hairbrush another way. After all, if she kept her hair short enough, she'd never need to brush it anyway.

As she dropped the last tangled curl down the toilet (well, why bother filling the bathroom bin? She'd only have to empty it herself), she gazed at the rejuvenated face in Bryan's shaving mirror and felt giddy with her new-found freedom.

She ate her breakfast standing up (a plain croissant, straight out of the packet without a plate), and looked at her watch. It was 7.45am. It was Tuesday. If Bryan had still been here, he'd have been putting out the recycling about now, carefully sorted into plastics, paper, glass and textiles. She went into the hall and slid back the bolt on the stair-cupboard, before remembering that, without Bryan there to sort out the recycling, there'd be nothing to put out. There stood Bryan's boxes, still lined up in a neat row, labelled and colour-coded (though surely the bin men could spot the difference between a bottle and a newspaper without his directions?) But the boxes were as empty as her days.

Shifting awkwardly in her slippers, Harriet hugged herself through her pyjama jacket as a single chilly tear rolled down her cheek. And yet...

She flicked on the understairs light – there was a single leaflet lying at the bottom of the box for paper. Could it possibly be a coded message from Bryan?

Harriet knew this was unlikely, but she couldn't get the thought out of her head unless she checked. As she stooped to pick up the leaflet, she felt a draught sneak up between her pyjama top and bottoms. The bright orange leaflet gleamed like a Belisha beacon beneath the stair cupboard's dim bulb.

Then she remembered: this was not a note, but a booklet that Bryan had pulled out of the letterbox and dropped in to the newly emptied paper recycling box, his final act before slipping away to the waiting car of his floozy. She hadn't looked at the boxes since, but now her attention was aroused.

"New term, new beginnings at Central College," announced the booklet's cover. "It's never too late to become what you've always wanted to be. Sign up now for an adult education course!"

With a sharp gasp of surprise, Harriet flipped over the page to find the index, where a whole new world lay before her. She ran a bitten fingernail down the course list, then on impulse closed her eyes and stopped her finger at random, pledging to take up as a hobby whatever course her finger had alighted on.

Here was a certain way to fill the void left by Bryan's departure. She opened her eyes to view what fate had in store.

Belly-dancing. Harriet smiled and hugged herself in delight. Now she really could let herself go.

.

Married Bliss

Henry and Lucinda have long realised that the most lasting manifestation of wedded bliss is not the kind that takes place behind closed doors. Instead they take more pleasure in sharing mundane everyday activities in full public view for which, strictly speaking, no marriage licence is required.

Accordingly, they set aside an hour every Sunday afternoon to flaunt the innocent, visible bonds that tie a couple together more certainly than ceremonial wedding vows.

They head into town to immerse themselves in crowds. Marketplaces; shopping centres; public parks; the zoo: strolling together through such settings endorses their intrinsic bond, the feeling that amid this sea of humanity they have singled out their soul-mate.

Forging their own little trail through swarms of shoppers and tourists, they are conscious of being a couple that conspicuously belongs together.

They don't need to speak to take comfort in each other's company. Just being in the same orbit fulfils them. A faint smile often plays about their lips as they wander along, side by side, though neither's said anything amusing nor so much as touched the other.

Wherever Henry and Lucinda stop for refreshments, the serving staff can tell at a glance that they're a couple. Occasionally one taking the order for drinks will ask Henry, "And for the wife?" but Lucinda never minds, despite her feminist principles.

Each Sunday afternoon outing ends the same way. Quietly they declare their love for each other before they peel off in a different direction into the crowd, without so much as a parting peck on the cheek.

Henry returns to his car, parked discreetly down a quiet alley, to begin his twenty-seven mile drive northward home. On his way he concocts the details of the day's fictitious snooker league match. He reports them to his wife Elaine when she's back from her bridge club. (In the early days, he'd used cricket matches as cover, but by the time the season was drawing to a close his affair with Lucinda had evolved into an all-year, all-weather addiction.)

Lucinda, meanwhile strolls back to the train station for the 4.32pm southbound service. Listlessly, she empties onto the concrete platform the water bottle she's meant to have drunk at Pilates. Watching the wet trail transform dusty ground into the colour of gleaming charcoal feels like a purging ceremony. She knows what she'll find on arriving home: her husband Michael and their grown-up sons, Ethan and Joe, snoozing off several pints taken after Sunday morning football matches. They'll only notice her absence if their dinner isn't ready when they awake. It will be. It always is.

But for just one stolen hour every Sunday, Henry and Lucinda enjoy their masquerade of
married bliss. And that one hour is all that either will have of it until they next meet.

Perfect Harmony

The moment her doorbell rang, Flora ran to the front door. She'd flung it wide open while the final chime was still resounding in the narrow hallway. In her haste to make William seem welcome, she allowed the doorknob to dent the anaglypta wallpaper. Never mind, she thought, not letting this little accident take the edge off her excitement. I'll coax it back into shape with a knitting needle after he's gone.

Too late, she realised that William would know from her speedy response that she'd been hovering at the front room window, looking out for him expectantly.

Her sallow face was unusually rosy, echoing the unflattering raspberry pink of her best cardigan. Before he'd even crossed the threshold, she blurted out an apology.

"I feel terrible for leaving it so long before calling you. I thought you'd be cross with me and would refuse to come. And the longer I left it, the worse I felt. Then I started to think that if I put it off much longer, we'd never be able to get it back to how it was - how it used to be - how it should be."

William took a conciliatory step towards her. One look at his long-lashed dark eyes compelled Flora to back up against the hallstand, where she stood shifting awkwardly from slippered foot to slippered foot. Her arms hung helplessly at her sides, surrendering, as she tried not to notice the hard umbrella handle pressing awkwardly against her coccyx from the hallstand.

"Don't think I hadn't been counting the months," he admonished her. "But I knew you'd call me in the end. You always do."

He closed the front door behind him. So masterful! thought Flora, eyeing his black pilot's case and familiar slender cane.

"Don't worry," he reassured her. "It would never be too late to pick up where we left off."

William hadn't been away so long that he'd forgotten the layout of her bungalow. He didn't need Flora to show him the way. Flora hung back, still penitent, as he strode confidently down the hall. Her recollection of his previous visit was as vivid as if it had been yesterday, but it seemed he had forgotten Flora's marmalade cat.

Suspicious of William's intentions, Robertson stood guarding the bedroom doorway, arching his back and hissing. Stirred into action by the sound, Flora scurried down the hall to catch up with them. Standing diplomatically between them both, she bent to smooth the cat's back, as if stroking down his anger-spiked fur would change his opinion of William.

"I'm sorry about Robertson," she said. "It's not that he doesn't like you, it's just the noises that you make. Cats have very sensitive hearing, you know."

Demonstrating his own repertoire of sounds, Robertson responded to Flora's touch with a purr reminiscent of a small food-mixer. But he didn't take his angry eyes off William, hoping to stare him out.

"But the noise doesn't bother me, you know." Flora gave a faint, nervous giggle. "In fact, I like them. They're all part of the experience. I look forward to it all, I really do."

William raised his eyebrows.

"Well, I won't hold back then."

As he threw open the last door, keen to get down to business, Flora brushed past him, making a bee-line for the net curtains, tugging at them to make sure they covered every last square inch of window pane. She didn't want anyone looking in from outside. She did not realise that no passer-by had ever assumed her life interesting enough to be worth spying on.

"Can I get you a cup of tea before you start?" she asked.

Was she playing for time, or just eager to please? William wondered. With two more women lined up for the afternoon, he could allocate her no longer than an hour. With a polite smile, he shook his head and set down his pilot case on the floor.

"No thanks. Let's just get on with it, shall we?"

Flora took his cane from his hand, scooped up his blazer as he shrugged it off, and lay them reverentially on the sofa. William rubbed his hands together, warming them ready for action. Flora hovered expectantly, watching his every move.

"As ever, I've come prepared," he assured her.

Slipping his hand into his trouser pocket, he pulled out a small silver tuning fork, turned his back and put his other hand out in front of him to feel his way.

"Now, let me at that lovely old piano."

With a yowl, the cat fled through the cat flap, while Flora, oblivious, settled back on the sofa, abstractedly stroking William's white stick.

Special Offer

I can't stand judgemental people, but if you tell me you've never taken an interest in other people's supermarket shopping trollies, I won't believe you. They're a snapshot of people's home lives, I tell you. And what better way to while away the time spent waiting in the checkout queue?

Show me the contents of a trolley, mid-shop, and I'll give you an identikit picture of the person pushing it. Weight, complexion, teeth, gait – you are what you eat, after all.

I just wish some of the plebs you see with trollies crammed with buy-one-get-one-free rubbish would look and learn from mine. It's a positive advertisement for healthy living.

Sometimes, I just want to grab some of these young mums by the arm and put them back on the straight and narrow. "Don't you know how many teaspoons of sugar there are in that can of pop?" I want to ask them. "And why buy white bread when you can have wholegrain?"

Not that they'd listen, of course. That's the trouble with young people today: too caught up in their own little world to see the bigger picture.

The snide old cow in front of me at the supermarket today really got my back up. Just because she could afford posh food (strawberries in February, for God's sake), she thought she had the right to sneer at the contents of other people's trollies. So what if that nice young piece was stocking up on iced doughnuts?

Still, I taught the old bat a lesson. While she was preoccupied with casting dirty looks at Miss BOGOF's shopping, I nicked her purse. Well, why buy one when you can get one free?

Autumn Leaves

Carefree, my small daughter Lucy and I are kicking up autumn leaves in the park when an elderly lady approaches, holding out a silver coin.

"I just found this shilling on the ground, dear. I'm giving it to you to bring you good luck."

Lucy does not realise that shillings haven't been legal tender for more than forty years. This coin is a modern ten pence piece.

"Thank you," says Lucy.

Smiling back, the elderly lady moves on in her own little world of five decades ago.

"She will need more luck in her autumn than we do," I murmur.

We are kinder to the leaves on our way home.

A Singular Life

At 11.11am every Thursday, Henry Williams, the old recluse from the end of the lane, makes his way to the village shop, clutching empty canvas bags held together by duct tape.

By 11.17am, his shopping bags are full. Every week he buys the same goods.

Unlike the villagers he meets, he never says hello.

In November, the shop closes, bankrupted by the superstore. Henry Williams cannot cope with catching a bus to town.

They find him, hypothermic, three weeks later, eating grass and leaves in his garden.

The ward manager makes him take a bath. She sees him as a surmountable challenge.

Henry Williams is not so sure.

Funeral March

For 17 years, Arnold Watson at 22 Kellaway Street and Derek Baker at number 26 had feuded over every neighbourly issue imaginable, from noise to parking to the clashing colours that they'd painted their front doors (one of them on purpose). Uncomfortably sandwiched at 24 was Clarrie Martin.

Clarrie was therefore surprised to notice Arnold creep in quietly at the back of the church, just before Derek was due to arrive by coffin.

A moment later, the *Funeral March* struck up, tremulous, on the church organ. Goodness, it was a while since she'd heard *that* played at a funeral, thought Clarrie. While she'd hardly expected Derek to plump for *Look on the Bright Side*, so popular at funerals these days, the opening bars of *My Way* would not have surprised her.

Or perhaps the *Funeral March* was the default if you didn't specify otherwise? Like the chirpy ringtone already set up on a new mobile phone. Clarrie tapped one brogued foot slowly in appreciation of the sombre rhythm.

She'd felt rather more like dancing in this last week since Derek had passed away. It was as if a weight had been lifted from her shoulders – or rather, her eardrums. Now that she no longer spent so much time with her hands over her ears to muffle his shouting, her knitting was coming along a treat.

The doctor said that Derek's death had been unexpected. Clarrie knew better. Watching his coffin progress slowly up the aisle on the shoulders of strangers, she speculated that Arnold failing to take in his recycling bin might count as the primary cause of Derek's death. Derek got almost as aerated over the binmen's schedule as Arnold did over Clarrie's cat digging up his garden.

As they strolled down the aisle to leave the church after the ceremony, Clarrie sidled up to Arnold, her sensible shoes crumpling the fake rose petals left on the ground from an earlier wedding. Ready to exchange the usual few hushed words in her special funeral voice, she was gratified to see that Arnold had been crying. Unclipping the gilt clasp of her shiny black funeral handbag, she drew out a floral scented tissue to offer him.

"There, there," she tremored, almost inaudibly. "I didn't realise you were so fond of poor Derek."

Arnold's whole body jolted towards her.

"Fond? FOND? What makes you think I was FOND?"

His words bounced off the ceiling of the near-empty church. Arnold didn't have a funeral voice.

"It just upsets me to think that one day it'll be ME up there in a wooden box. Bloody Derek, always had to have the last word!"

Clarrie stared.

"And by the way, Miss Martin, it's about time you trimmed your front hedge!"

Turning his back abruptly, Arnold marched off towards his car, elbowing the vicar, who was standing in the church porch, hand outstretched for post-funeral shaking purposes, out of his way.

Bound for home on the bus ten minutes later, Clarrie made a mental note to replace the shrinking pack of tissues when she got home. It was always good to keep your funeral handbag well stocked, she thought, brightening. You never knew when you might need it next. She'd better put the cat out too.

The Comfort of Neighbours

Maureen nudged Dorothy as they neared the recently widowed Sheila's house. Her elbow barely dented her friend's thick tweed coat. ("This'll see me out" had been Dorothy's justification for the extravagant purchase seven years before.)

"Of course, she'll have to take care of that big garden all on her own now, poor soul," said Maureen in a low voice.

Dorothy nodded thoughtfully.

"Good thing Isaac died in the autumn, when everything'll stop growing for a bit. She'll be able to break herself in gently, that's one blessing at least. Poor Sheila."

They shook their heads pityingly, then gazed straight ahead up the street until they were safely past Sheila's house. They were relieved that they'd managed not to bump into her since Isaac had died, as they had no idea what to say.

"Still, it must be hard, having to sweep up all those leaves on her own," Maureen continued, once they were safely beyond Sheila's house. "Even if nothing's growing, there's always dead leaves to get rid of."

If Maureen and Dorothy could have seen beyond the high fence around Sheila's back garden, they'd have realised that Sheila wasn't bothered by dead leaves. In fact, she was enjoying sweeping them into a big pile at the centre of the lawn. But it wasn't just the leaves that were destined for her bonfire. Beside the red petrol canister was a wheelbarrow overflowing with Isaac's possessions. All his favourite things were there: that filthy pipe; the dreadful stuffed owl; the tatty old slippers she was always falling over. One at a time, she flung these items on top of the mound of leaves and thought of all the beautiful ash that the conflagration would create. Afterwards, the ash would be invaluable in helping her prepare a soft fruit bed on the spot that Isaac had used to grow dahlias for the last thirty-two years.

Dahlias – now there was something else that Sheila couldn't abide.

She twisted off the top of the petrol canister, doused the mound with a sprinkle of fuel to get it started, and struck a match. Finally she would be free.

Thank you for reading QUICK CHANGE.

If you enjoyed it, please consider
posting a brief review online
or recommending the book to your friends.

Every review will help other readers find this book.
It will also make the author's day!

Bonus Material

This new paperback edition of *Quick Change* includes two additional short stories that do not feature in the original ebook: *Upwardly Mobile* and *Please Remain Silent*.

Both of these stories were inspired by public libraries, and were chosen for flash fiction anthologies.

Upwardly Mobile

Every other Tuesday, halfway through my shift in the village shop, I'd watch the white mobile library bus trundle past on its way to park by the village school. On its return trip twenty minutes later, the lady driver would wave cheerfully to me. In our narrow lane, the giant books painted on the side of the van almost touched the shop window, making me feel the size of a Borrower, which was ironic, because I'd never borrowed any of its books.

Then, at the start of October, my hours at the shop were cut. Our takings had been falling since the new superstores popped up a few miles away. After that, I was always at home on Tuesdays. Alone in my cottage opposite the school, I'd watch the library van park outside my house.

As soon as its doors swung open, schoolchildren bearing books would bound up its steps. Older folk followed more slowly, cautiously gripping the handrail with their book-free hand. When they emerged, one by one, they'd all be smiling, large print books a common bond between the very old and the very young.

As the days shortened, I grew weary of daytime television. I wished I could afford more bus trips into town or to anywhere that would make my life less dull. Then last Tuesday afternoon, I finally found my courage. Once its regular visitors had dispersed, I slowly mounted the mobile library's steps.

"Can I help you, dear?" asked the lady driver, now standing behind the counter. It seemed odd to hear her voice at last.

"I don't know," I faltered. "You see, I'm not much of a reader."

When she ducked behind the counter, I thought it was to hide her scorn, but she popped up again with a library card application form and a pen.

"Ooh, everyone's a reader, dear!" she exclaimed kindly. "You just haven't round the right books yet. We've got something here for everyone. I'll help you choose."

But that's all I have time to tell you now, because I want to get back to my book.

This story was especially written for the anthology in which it first appeared in 2014. **Change the Ending - Stories that matter: flash fiction about the future of public life** *was curated by Dawn Reeves and published by Shared Press.*

Please Remain Silent for the Benefit of Other Library Users (In Hushed Tones)

Why, Miss Blossom, how lovely to see you back in the Reading Room, it's been a while, has it not? I hope you've been keeping well. *The Times*? Yes, I've finished with *The Times*. Please be my guest. No, no, I've definitely finished.

I was just going to toddle along to the Science section until I saw you. Yes, Neuroscience, actually, it's a new interest of mine. I've been spending a lot of time in that department lately. Fascinating stuff, absolutely fascinating.

Just yesterday, I came across a fact I'd never known before. Tell me, have you ever noticed that although the smell of polish hits you the minute you enter the library, you cease to notice it after a while? Apparently, that's nature's way. We're all programmed to stop noticing a smell, good or bad, within moments of first sensing it. Yes, unpleasant smells too. Yes, I suppose it is a blessing. That must be why that air freshener company has been advertising a device that alternates between two different perfume reservoirs – so that the user is constantly reminded that it's working.

No, no, I don't watch much commercial television either. I just happened to switch over by mistake.

But the same applies to all the other senses, according to the book I've been reading over in the Science section. If you hear a sound repeatedly, it fades into the background. Yes, trains passing your flat at night, that's an excellent example. You only notice them when they stop – when there's a strike and they don't run. I've noticed that too. You're so right. Next time I'm kept awake by the cessation of striking trains, I shall – there, I shall say it! – I shall think of you.

And have you noticed how the same food or drink, day after day, ceases to be pleasurable? Yes, that first cup of proper English tea after a trip abroad is always the best, you're quite right.

And as to touch, well, I never notice the cat curled up against my arm on the bed at night, once she and I have settled down. Your cat sleeps on your bed too? Sooty sleeps on your bed, curled up into the small of your back? Oh, Miss Blossom, I say! I wonder whether our cats would be friends if they met?

The other sense? The fifth one? Does it work for the sense of sight? Well, do you know, I am at odds with the book on that one. Because, Miss Blossom, because – and I don't care if the librarian is looking daggers at me since you ask – no matter how often I spot you in this Reading Room, and no matter how long I gaze at you before you look up and notice me, I will never tire of the sight of you. Oh Miss Blossom, dare I ask? Would you care to join me for the afternoon in the Science Section?

This story was selected for inclusion in **Eating My Words - The National Flash Fiction Day 2014 Anthology**, *edited by Calum Kerr, Angela Readman and Amy Mackelden, published by Gumbo Press.*

Acknowledgements

Thank you to Calum Kerr, founder of National Flash Fiction Day, and other flash authors who inspired me to write this book, especially Helena Mallett and Bart van Goethem. Thanks also to my author friends within the Alliance of Independent Authors who are always so supportive, especially Orna Ross and Karen Lotter.

Huge thanks to my wonderful beta readers, all authors themselves: Lucienne Boyce, Elizabeth Eyles, Marius Gabriel, Mari Howard, Georgia Rose and Pip Westgate. Special thanks to Lucienne for pointing out my obsession with recycling bins, which now appear in fewer stories!

I'm very grateful to my editor Alison Jack for her meticulous work, and to SilverWood Books for their guidance on cover design.

I'd be in big trouble if I didn't acknowledge the moral support of my husband Gordon and daughter Laura while I wrote into the night, and my family for making me the sort of person capable of writing a book like this. I'd like to assure my brother and sister that the episode in "Going to Grandma's" in which I cheerfully concuss the narrator's older siblings is not really Freudian wish-fulfilment.

Debbie Young

To find out more about Debbie Young's books and writing life,

check out her author website:

www.authordebbieyoung.com

where you can also join her free mailing list

to be kept informed via email

about her new books and public events

Lightning Source UK Ltd.
Milton Keynes UK
UKOW04f0225270315

248626UK00002B/26/P